Fanny H.R. Poole

A Bank of Violets

Fanny H.R. Poole

A Bank of Violets

ISBN/EAN: 9783337123291

Printed in Europe, USA, Canada, Australia, Japan

Cover: Foto ©Andreas Hilbeck / pixelio.de

More available books at **www.hansebooks.com**

A BANK OF VIOLETS

VERSES BY

FANNY H. RUNNELLS POOLE

G. P. PUTNAM'S SONS

NEW YORK
27 West Twenty-third Street

LONDON
24 Bedford Street, Strand

The Knickerbocker Press

1895

The Knickerbocker Press, New York

O, it came o'er my ear like the sweet south,
That breathes upon a bank of violets.

                    Duke Orsino in "Twelfth Night."

Were Poetry the sweet south breeze,
   To breathe upon my violets,
Delight would thrill the neighboring trees
Of Helicon ; and Fancy ease
   Her heart in far-heard triolets,
Were Poetry the sweet south breeze
   To breathe upon my violets !

                                F. H. R. P.

iii

TO ETHEL

Of late when in a May walk's resting-space,
    I placed you on a knoll of budding green,
Impressioned on your brightly-answering face,
    Slept the calm air, the scene ;

Till wonderingly your wee, expectant hands
    Alit like new-embodied butterflies
And shone your eyes on violet-drifted sands,
    In gladdest baby-wise.

May time restore to you that perfect hour !
    In some fair future, haply may you trace
Some faint and fleeting beauty in each flower
    Herein, with loving grace.

MID-MAY, 1893.

CONTENTS

CONTENTS

AMONG FRIENDS

CONTENTS

FAITH

Partly Fancy

O Fancy, if thou flyest, come back anon,
Thy fluttering wings are soft as love's first word !

—JEAN INGELOW.

PRELUDES

I

O FEARLESS little brook, fling out your utmost forces,
The greening cresses hasten at your shining hem !
Beside, that every heart may drink joy at its sources,
Bid all fair weeds come forth to our full need of them !

II

And Robin, is it you whose song comes up the hollow ?
Trill upon trill, a song whose meaning I would follow,

Again as when a child, full wond'ringly I listen,

While o'er the timid grass the tears of April
glisten ;

The clouds bend low in sorrow ;

Loved Robin, that you borrow

Joy from the darksome day wherewith to bid
" Good-morrow ! "

III

Sweet is the sound of Spring to the heart wintry
and waiting,

Sweet, ah sweet !

Blithe from the building nest is the Robin's note
in mating,

Sing, for there 's never a space for sighing or for
hating,

Sing and repeat !

4

Fleet is the round of joy in the Spring hours
gayly flying,
Fleet, ah fleet !
Up and follow the breeze ere its buoyant pulse
be dying,
Sing, for there 's never a space for hating or for
sighing,
Sing and repeat !

JUNE

NORTHERN May's a coy, sweet maiden,
  Blithe of voice, arbutus-laden,
But the beauty that we seek is beauty's queen ;
  She will tune our hearts to singing,
  Melodist of joy up-winging,
We will know her for her breath is eglantine !

  When the royal earth discloses
  Her fond heart in giving roses,
And the thrush and swallow warble all in tune,
  And the hill and meadow smiling
  Beckon us with looks beguiling,
Then from Orient (or Eden) comes the June !

  Foam and wave, O emerald grasses,
  Make a pathway as she passes !
List, how madly wings the bluebird far and near
  With the tune we can but capture !—
  'T is the universal rapture,
And a *June, of queens the fairest, June is here !*

BEAUTY

I

I THOUGHT on Beauty, but could not con-
     tain
   My soul, her limit or infinity !
   Methought, *Where she is not*, reveal to me,
Conceive her utmost bound my soul would fain !
In mountain solitudes she roams unbound,
Her breath but stirs the brook and it is given
To curvèd smile and keen delight of sound.
While in untrodden fastnesses, rock-riven,
   She reigns, august in splendor, far and lone,
   Surmised of, yet except in dream unknown.

II

In the immeasurable shadows of the hills
   Are undulant, dream-tranquil intervales,

7

BEAUTY

Wherein to muse, this raptured heart regales,
Till all forgot are life's encircling ills. . . .
The afterglow, the twilight and the dew
Of unworn even pass before me now,
And Nature's soul of sweetness me doth woo ;
Her nectared breath, dusk form and star-lit
     brow
     Would beckon me unto the Life Ideal,
     Thro' Beauty's ministry, divinely real.

A MARÉCHAL NIEL ROSE

WOULDST thou to some lone triumph
    marshal us—
  Some sphere of endless sun
Above dim death—some Eden marvellous—
  Thou dauntless one ?

For Rose, succeeding him whose name thou
    hast,
  Thou couldst not brook defeat,
In our heart's Solferino win at last
  Victory complete !

THE HEART OF A ROSE

WHO knows the inmost heart of a rose,
  Treasure hidden of sun and dew?—
Knows ere the wizard June unclose
  Her magical meaning, who?
  Ere the lightsome, eager wind doth woo
And waft her fragrance, heart of a rose
    Who knows?

Altho' in my heart thy beauty grows,
  Purely, my Love, and still more true,
Not yet of thy deepest heart disclose,
  Till I, of the longing view,
  May wear thee worthily, without rue,
My June—the fairest that nature knows—
    My Rose!

THE BOBOLINKS

THE buoyant music of the bobolinks
    Outpours upon the June ;
Now is the high-tide of the year, methinks,
  With love and joy atune !
      Yet more, I ween,
      Than heard or seen,
Is that which back to fancy brings
The presence of remembered things.
The air is filled with melody,
And so, my heart, with memory !

Once more and now, O playmate of my choice,
  Only to live is sweet !
Thro' the billowy open floats your voice,
  Too happy at your feet,

11

Kingcups, daisies,
In grassy mazes,
Sway low at your undulant tread ;
Hush ! you are calling, " Just ahead,
Something soft to keep and to hold,
Hurry ! all ebony and gold,

"On the brier-rose, there ! O Constantin "—
But off with arrowy flight,
Never a moment our grasp within,
Gleameth a ray of light,
Its way along
A daring song ! . . .
Ah well ! adown these after-years,
Fair is the gold and few the tears.
Playmates, we follow yet—and then
Here are the bobolinks again !

DREAM-WINGS

A CHILD — untrammelled curtains of the
sun fall o'er it
In shimmering folds, brown hands reach tire-
lessly before it
  To gain, on restless wing
  Yon transitory thing;
  Believing one, agleam
With hope, fast-flying now behold it,
Your eager palm cannot enfold it,
  'T is but a dream.

Sweet tearful child, we feared in vain that you
would chase it,
We lost a full hour yestermorn, who can re-
place it?
  And butterflies, and bright romances,
  The fairest are uncaptured fancies,
  Are but a dream!

" I HAVE had joy in life," she said, " and
   sweet protection
  Of shielding arms, since o'er my sheltered
   way
A mother's holy presence and supreme affection
  Passed to be Memory's divinest ray.

" O yet new bliss ! my child's pure love to keep
   the sky bright "—
She paused. An angel with melodious breath
Whisp'ring, drew o'er her eyes the soft, cool
   touch of twilight,
  " I too am Love, but men have called me
   Death."

A PERI

O H, to dream by this dappled stream,
  Tuned to thy rune, æolian beeches !
Low the rioting sunbeam reaches,
Chasing the trout with wanton gleam.
High in the boughs a thrush is hidden,
Voicing a rapture free, unbidden.

Save the stray angler passing just without—
  His pathway tracked where coverts lure the
    rod—
None other wanders.   Wild azaleas nod,
And grudging not, give their heart-perfume out.
How deftly moss and clematis do drape
This tempting couch the tangled oak-roots
    shape !

Full happiness in life doth here abide.

    Such fragrant calm imparts the wilding grape,
Would it might penetrate yon hovel-side !—
What joy, what hope one woman might betide,
Haply to stitch, throughout stern morrows,
Something—not hunger's garb, nor sorrow's !

LOVE'S JEWEL

HOLD this opal to the light,
  Maiden, each tint glows—
  Violet and rose,
Flame of ruby, diamond white.

I can see at clearest view
  Your pure heart, beside,—
  Each fond charm denied
Save to one who 's nearest you.

SONG AND MEMORY

OH, song for the sadness of life
    As for the bird its wings !
But oh, my heart, that bears a dart
    For beauty of past things !—
For the gleam of a vanished day,
    A far-receding shore,
The sweetness of a rhythmic lay
    That fills the soul no more.

One haunting face of other-while,
    The passion of a tear,
Remembered radiance of a smile
    That now suns other sphere ;
A half-revealèd, shy caress,
    The magic of a word,
The flutter of a faded tress,
    By breath of fancy stirred.

Oh, Song for the sorrow of life,
   As for the bird its wings !
But why, my heart, to bear a dart
   For beauty of past things ?
Such vital joys can never die,
   They are as hope to love,
They sing themselves in Memory
   As angels sing above.

A CONTRAST

DORIS at the piano, so eager, with eyes a-
glisten,

Bent on a witching melody, pauses a space to
listen,

Just outside in the madcap wind the branches
moan and shiver,

All thro' the storm-blown dell comes the driven
spray of the river.

Everything 's bright within. Life leaps in a
keen desire !

Grandchild Ruth with her quaint doll-wisdom
regales the Squire,

Youth makes swift to explore the beautiful, wise
and strange,

Art and science lure the mind on their unbounded range.

Brother Ralph for the nonce surrenders his
    geometric plan,
When a Viking shouts from his blazoned niche,
    " Draw me, if you can ! "
While Doris, speeding the attack by a storm of
    thrilling sound,
Wakes at the fireside citadel the faithful, dream-
    eyed hound.

Thus as the storm-king rideth the night that
    heavily trembles,
Stepping within, methinks the scene a heav'n of
    joy resembles ;
One with Doris and Ralph, attune I gladness for
    Nature's weeping,
Leaving the unsolved problem of life to God's
    most gracious keeping !

A PERSIAN EPISODE

VIOLET :

AH me ! sits he within the oaken chair,
    Deep-buried in a tale of Persian lore ?
Or at the easel-shrine doth he recline,
Scanning a wood-nymph sweet beyond compare ?
My lord, whose nearness makes the day divine,
I see him thro' the jealous-guarding door.

Oh, if I were an houri, lotus-fair,
I would steal in, as wave upon the shore,
To clasp him ! and arise incarnadine,
As 't were from out that mystic-breathing prayer,
The *Yazna*, which amid the *Zend* doth shine ;
(He would not marvel, and I glad him more.)

Nay, nay ! to break the charm I should not dare,
Over the *Zend-Avesta* he doth pore ;
A few weeks since, he said my eyes were wine,
And now, grown picturesque in my despair,

Beside his name I stitch a silk *Gulnare.*

Too-happy scarf of sheen ! for you will twine

Around my *hakim ;* he will understand

And think me——

ROB :

Violet ! Violet, where are you ?

Prithee, leave broider-work and come to me !

Copy this treatise in your firm, clear hand,

The publisher may then more plainly see

The beauties of the doctrine, brought to view,

Of Zoroaster——Why, my sweet, 't is true,

You grieve. What, tears ? Yes, heavily the dew

Doth shroud my Violet. It gives me pain.

And why ? I do insist, pray, Love, explain ;

I cannot bear it,—if you weep, woe 's me !

VIOLET *(sobbing) :*

O Rob, you are so noble—

learn'd and grand—

If I—were—Zoroaster—I might gain—
Your love—for which I long—to-day—in
    vain—
Because—I love you !

ROB *(enclasping her) :*

       Is that all ?   My own !
Why he, poor fellow, is a great unknown !
Believe me, I declare——

VIOLET :

       Well——

ROB :

       On the strand
The breeze comes tenderly.   Let 's walk alone.
                 (Exeunt.)

BERNARD DE VENTADOUR

1169

SHINE out in mediæval lore,
  In proud chateau and abbey hoar,
Like violets on a barren moor,
The love-lays of the troubadour,
      Bernard de Ventadour.

'Mid kingly wrath and feudal wrong,
In truth what lives so sweet as song?
What knight but finds his fairest prize
In love-light of his lady's eyes?
And doughty deeds may well enhance
Acceptance of the fair one's glance,
While, for the kiss withholden long,
Thy pleading eloquence of song,
      Bernard de Ventadour.

If thou be fled, we follow thence
Thy peerless witchery, Provence !
As the inrushing years full sweet
The miracle of morn repeat,
From love's unquiet gloom not less
Spring fire and strength and tenderness.
And we would speed a shaft of song
To quell the indefinable wrong,
Perchance to glad the world once more—
Our Agnes and our Eleanore,
Thro' smile or scorn, undaunted, sure,
While love and life and time endure,
Like thee, O sage and troubadour,
　　　　　Bernard de Ventadour !

DAPHNE

WHEN comes the drowsy milking-time,
    Beside a sweet-breathed cow
She sits, the Daphne of my rhyme,
    With grave but winsome brow.
The redbreast calls his happy mate,
    The partridge sounds his drum,
While 't is for Daphne's smile sedate
    That hillward I am come ;
And if my love I cannot speak,
    'T is she who knows the whole,
Oh, 't is the blush on Daphne's cheek
    That lingers in my soul.

And Oh, to win her love I 'll dare,
    Whoe'er may chide or chaff me !
It 's moonlight fair and fresh the air,
    And o'er the hills to Daphne !

One eve a kiss I did surprise ;
   Sure, I had guessed her then,
But no, there 's magic in her eyes
   Not read of gods or men.
I wonder not I often sigh,
   A-following my teams,
To think that such a bore as I
   Should dare disturb her dreams !
All round Chocorua's friendly peak
   The dazzling sun-clouds roll,
But 't is the blush on Daphne's cheek
   That burns into my soul.

The village lads—because she 's not
   For them, they oft will chaff me,
But be my lot a simple cot
   And long sweet life with Daphne !

LAKE WINNIPISEOGEE

WE know not which is fairer, the repose
Of verdured islands, or the tremulous
foam
That guards them, as the ancients cradled
Rome—
Cherished in splendor. To the heights gleam
those
Majestic sentinels that silence knows
And the proud heavens ;—Chocorua's lofty
home,
Ossipee, Whiteface, Belknap's double dome,
Lone Washington and Lafayette, where glows
A grandeur that exceedeth mortal ken.
Lake of the hills, thou art the link to bind
Yon mountains and our souls! thy beating breast,
Less equable, endears the humble mind ;
For had ye, Hills, no human bond confest,
Ye were the shrine of gods and not of men !

IN THE CEMETERY AT FRANKFORT

I WANDER in a city, tranquil, fair,
   Upon whose towers the sun's departing
      beam
Betokens the sweet bound of mortal care ;
   Below, the music of a winding stream,
Above, birdsongs in the dream-laden air,
   And still above, blue heavens of which we
      dream,
And souls of them who sleep the glory wear.

They sleep, to wake unfettered of the clay—
   Dear forms who bore unknown life's better
      part
And softly stole upon the heavenly way ;
   The brave, enshrined within the nation's
      heart—

Are they unmindful of our love to-day?
   Each soul, well-rounded howsoe'er thou art,
Eternity be good to thee, we pray.

I wander in a city, tranquil, fair,
   I can but think, of all earth's joy 't were best
To sleep amid so much of beauty there,
   Resigning all on Nature's tender breast,
Far from the strife of worlds that do and dare,
   O blest foreshadow of most perfect rest!
O heights of God, the soul's eternal share!

THE LATE YEAR

SAD is the vanishing year,
But sweet her farewell glancing.
Oh, the squirrel chirps good cheer
From his full granary dancing,
His conscious head a-toss ;
He knows all ruddy mirth,
But not the pain of loss.
She 's weary—the gray old earth.
Sing ho, and fair be her dreaming !

Sweet the ling'ring scent of flowers,
But sad their vacant places,
Oh, the browning woodland bowers
Laugh with jubilant faces ;—
The frisk hare and field mouse,
And otter near the brook,
The newly-feathered grouse
With his wise, prophetic look,
Sing ho, for the warm life teeming !

Oh, the downy, drifted ground,—
  Shy, furry folk they delve it,
And often tread a gay round
  As 't were on princely velvet,
Between the frosty boughs
  The amber sunset glows,
Such wealth the day allows,
  On, on to its starry close !
Sing ho, the exultant gleaming !

It is only we who yield
  Sorrow the parting season,
The simple life of the field
  Hath instinct 'bove our reason ;
On such the snow doth fall—
  Joy's benedicite,
But Spring's inspiring call
  For the souls that dream with me !
Sing ho, and fair be the dreaming !

Among Friends

Neither is life long enough for friendship ; that is a serious and majestic affair.

—RALPH WALDO EMERSON.

REALITY

WHAT joy to breathe the air by thee made
    sweet,
  To tread the woodland ways by thee made
    dear!
  Almost I fear me, trembling, art thou here—
Lurks here the rhythmic cadence of thy feet?
With what a pure, proud rapture wouldst thou
    greet
  Me as of old! Yet for the whelming tear,
  The rush of blissful pain to feel thee near,
I scarce could brook thine ardent eyes to meet.

Forgive, dear heart, alone is mine the blame;
  E'en to the over-world, thou like a star
    Doth rise to claim the homage of my heart;
What though unsought, O claimant, be thy
    claim!
  Thou reignest o'er my life from realms afar,
    Inspirer of my nature and my art!

AN EIGHTY-SIXTH BIRTHDAY

TO H. S. B., JUNE 1, 1883

TO one whose long and busy years
    Count many a noble action done,
Who in the race of life appears
    Victor, with triumphs bravely won,
And triumphs yet to win are thine,
Ere victor's crown upon thee shine.

For steadfast souls the world hath room,
    Them, flatt'ring fortune cannot foil,
Such souls are sunlight to the gloom ;
    Are sinew to the arm of toil ;
Are to the suffering friend no less
That they themselves have earned success.

Such is thy life, O brave and fair !
    And thou, upheld by love and truth,

AN EIGHTY-SIXTH BIRTHDAY

Dost ever in a world of care
   Maintain thy gladsome heart of youth—
A heart that winter may not guess,
But fraught with June's own loveliness!

While peerless June on either hand,
   Proclaims the joy-time of the year,
Laden with goodly bloom, how grand
   Thy six and eighty years appear!
As June with flowers, so is thy life
Fragrant of deeds with kindness rife.

And when thy heart shall cease to beat—
   The life that dawned with dawning June
When ceased—what memory more sweet,
   To aching hearts what richer boon,
Than that each coming June shall start
Some fresh remembrance of thine heart?

IN HER ALBUM

STILL go thy way, sweet friend,
    Garner rich thoughts to lend
Food to the fainting, vision to the blind !
Finding all beauty where thy footsteps tend,
    " Haunted forever by the eternal Mind."

A MARRIAGE MORN

TO H. N. K.

WELCOME to this thrice happy morn,
The gladdest of a glad young life,
Since first it breathes with joy new-born
The hallowed name of wife!

Heaven's richest gifts be ever strown,
And flowers of purity and truth
For her who linketh with thine own
The beauty of her youth.

Unfold in beauty, hills and fields,
Beam forth in light, in bloom and song!
While earth her fairest foliage yields
And bright hours speed along.

Unite thy radiance with the sky,
  'Thou earth, so old yet ever young !
Let love be twofold melody,
  Be twofold bridals sung !

Let the stern years, a motley throng,
  Unbroken find thy dream of bliss,
Find the old love still ever strong—
  A world outlasting this.

A CHILD OF SUMMER

'TWAS in the time of golden-rod,
    When o'er the woodland's changing green
    A faint September blush is seen,
When up and down the teeming sod
Tawn bees are clover-banqueting,
When swallows mount on Southward wing,
When latest Summer's winy cheer
Uplifts the full heart of the year.

Just in the year's enchanted prime,
    An angel with invisible wings,
    Fairer than all imaginings,
She came, and set our lives to rhyme.
Starred with grave wonder, shy surprise,
Shone clear the midnight of her eyes,
And there suffused her face swart gleams
Of lately-hovering tropic dreams.

Now, longer strayed from that far land
    Where Summer doth not bid adieu,
    Still to her birthright is she true,
A wood-nymph—lingers in her hand
The goddess Summer's ardent touch,
Summer leans to her overmuch ;
She hath the haunting croon of brooks
Subdued in leafy, slumbering nooks.

She knows the mystic harmonies—
    Composite music of the breeze
    At play thro' silver birchen trees—
And oft her voice doth echo these,
For her, grow soft the tones of birds,
That she may comprehend their words,
She knows the twinkling showers that pass,
The wind that waves the upland grass.

Thro' storm and calm of seasons' change,
    Companioned still by Summer's grace,

A CHILD OF SUMMER

About her fresh and radiant face
The purest fancies charmèd range.
God grant no cloud of doubt may dim
His child's unbounded faith in Him,
Nor ever sorrow, nor unrest
Make her less summer-fair and blest !

IN AUTUMN

HAST thou forgotten, heart of love,
   How fair the beauty fled,
That thou dost see around, above,
   The glory of the dead—
The passing splendor that must only
Desert us, thus bereft and lonely ?

Thou Friend who fadest from my clasp !
   Around me blossometh
Thy greatness, my poor mind would grasp,
   Thy very life in death !
Let past be past ; I can but guess thee,
'T is Nature's self who doth confess thee !

TO THE LYRIST OF "LET THE DREAM GO"

ANNE REEVE ALDRICH

NOT as an infant, reaching timid hands
　　To unknown darkness, didst thou greet
　　　the lands
Lit by the wisdom of thy heart and brain,
Foreseen and sung by sight and music fain,
　　　With faith's own clearness
　　　And loving nearness
Breathing throughout thy message unmistaken.

Pure heart, by death not crushed, nor even
　　　shaken,
Only hast left the song-lit halls awhile
Where I yet pause, remembering thy smile,
Remembering the radiance of thy face,
Knowing thine echoed voice, thy spirit's grace.

Thee did Thought's couriers hail on restless
    feet—
Their hope, their joy to me thou didst repeat.
Then camest Death, even with feet of love![1]
Who said that thou art dead? Hark, from
    above
        Floats some rich thought of thine
        To other hearts than mine!
So fair thy life, enthroned in memory so,
Who evermore couldst let the bright dream go?

[1] *The Feet of Love* is the name of a novel written by
Miss Aldrich.

AFTER READING "SPAIN AND THE SPANIARDS"

TO EDMONDO DE AMICIS

I

WE thank thee, O traditioner and sage
    Worthy of Marco Polo and his land,
  Dispenser of delight, at whose command
Grave History unfolds a glowing page !
Caliph and odalisque, of some dim age,—
    King, painter, poet pass—a stately band—
    Zorilla, Espronceda, and the grand
Cervantes who inspires our noble rage.

Ourselves we 'd barter for a lightsome rover
In many-mosqued and rose-perfumed Cordova,
Stray Andalusian airs anon to hear

The while we sail the fair Guadalquiver !

By gay kiosk, by Moorish palaces,

High-towered Seville and dazzling-white Cadiz.

II

O tireless traveller, we follow thee

    Where dreamed the great Columbus with the

        eyes

    Far-seeing, which divined a New World rise !

Deep in that old Sevillian library

Felt he the deathless honors yet to be.

    We too, with growing tenderness would prize

    The annotations masterful and wise

Upon this parchment rich with prophecy !

Bright roamer, friend, we cherish thy impres-

    sions,

To all brave deeds our soul would make con-

    fessions,

Till truth and beauty into being grow
Bold with Velasquez, calm with Murillo. . . .
Speed on ! E'en while th' Alhambra charms
    our view,
Thoughts of Columbus shape our life anew !

ON READING "UNDERWOODS"

And strains there are
That whoso hears shall hear for evermore.
—ROBERT LOUIS STEVENSON.

SOMETIME ago 'mid Underwoods I pon-
dered,
Feeding upon the morn,
While from fields newly shorn
Fragrant south winds round me dreamily wan-
dered.

Somewhere made melody
A trancèd spirit,
Ever I hear it
Stilling life's threnody.

Was 't the voice of the hermit thrush? I pon-
dered,
Or likewise, pure, apart,
Stevenson's boundless art?
When amid "Underwoods" charm-bound I
wandered.

IN THE GARDEN OF KEATS

" I can feel the flowers growing over me," Keats said to
a friend in his last springtime.

SUCH wealth of Poetry divine
    Doth ease love's darkling sorrow.
Then, primrose, ope thy sunlit hope,
    For joy doth wait the morrow !

Pass classic shapes of quiet bliss,
    Passes to dream, Endymion.
Then back to Truth, O beauteous Youth,
    Call thy *reveille* clarion !

Ah, Heaven, that not to him the winds
    Might whisper thy foreknowing,
Deathless the bays of love and praise
    My Keats felt o'er him growing !

THE POET OF JUNE

WILLIAM CULLEN BRYANT

THOU Poet, crowned with song's supremest
   powers,
  Who, in that realm from pain and death apart,
  Dost link, responsive to our longing heart,
The infinite with some stray chord of ours !

As waiting nature greets the wondrous showers
   Bidding a barren earth in beauty start,
   Oh, would that we, by thine inspiring art,
Might weave thee garlands eloquent in flowers !

And June is here, Interpreter who fled,
Her halo still upon thy laurelled head
   To be divinely bright while ages roll ;
Thy pure eyes glow a June-day's temperate fire,
A June *adagio* sweeps thy " living lyre,"
   With stately rapture to enthrall our soul !

HAIL AND FAREWELL!

MAKE the hours jocund with rout and was-
    sail,
    The goodly board heap high !
My fancy it paints a gleaming castle
    Where fairest life flits by,
Where youths and maidens foot it madly
    Under the mistletoe ;
The Old Year joins the mirth right gladly
    There 's minstrelsy, but Oh,
When comes the young day 't will be sung or
    said :
All hail to the blithe and kingly comer,
But here 's a sigh for the Year that is fled !

Oh, a knightly train, with old-time graces
    Sweeps o'er the palace floor,
With high-born beauty and flower-sweet faces ;
    Us they may charm no more !

There 's the gay jester, Joy-in-despair,
　　Slain of a broken heart ;
But heavenly Charity lingers there,
　　(Hers is a deathless part).
List, while at the dawn 't will be sung or said :
　All hail to a blithe and kingly comer,
But here 's a sigh for the Year that is fled !

Hey the New Year, the frolicsome fellow !
　　Pleasure his reign foretells,
Pledge him the wassail, fruity and mellow,
　　Pledge—Hark, the chime of bells !
Ah ! when our dream of life is ended—
　　Lost in the Higher Will,
May one fond heart we have befriended
　　Hold us in memory still !
At morn may it one time be sung or said :
　Love will yet be, Joy, a frequent comer,
But here 's a sigh for the friend who is fled !

Faith

Still shall I climb,

Even though the stars shine not on my steep way ;

Sometime—sometime—

That upland I will gain, and find the day.

—ROBERT BURNS WILSON.

SERVICE

NOT in the possibilities of power,
　　Nor grand, vague theories of truth and
　　　right,
　Not what were ours had we attained the
　　height
Of culture, wisdom-crowned, with art a-flower,
Nay ! but the service of the present hour
　　Enlists us, claims our life's supremest might ;
　　In what we are is triumph or delight,
　In what we are lies our immortal dower.

And it is glorious—this gift of life,
More glorious that He, the chiefest man,
　　Forsook heaven's throne to tread these human
　　　ways.
His the high passion, His the nobler strife
Shaping and strengthening our spirit's plan ;
　　To us perfected life, to Him the praise !

"ONE THING I DO"

"I press on toward the goal, unto the prize of the high calling of God in Christ Jesus."

SAINT PAUL, thy ringing words shall rouse
    the soul
  To all brave action! Nobler far the strife
Shall be accounted to attain the goal
  Of Christian truth, than to devote this life
To fame's achievement, or some worldly prize.
  Still Godward shall the mark of manhood
    rise.

"One thing I do"—how few of us can say—
  Amid the checkered toil of brain and hand,
The fall of high ideals, and the sway
  Of masters who feel not, nor understand,
The many feeble and the mighty few,
  Who lives can truly say, "One thing I do"?

"ONE THING I DO"

And yet 't is possible, O heavenly thought,

    Life-giving hope, the soul's enduring test !—

To keep the faith for which th' apostles fought,

    And afterward receive their blessed rest.

Through persecutions let the echo roll—

    "One thing I do, I press on toward the goal ! "

REFLECTIONS

I

UNCONSCIOUSLY we write upon our faces
 The feeling and the fancy of the hour,
Whether our hearts possess love's kindred
  graces,
  Or hatred's power.

Whether our lives are broadened by brave
  daring—
 Strife against sin and selfish, sordid greed,
Or hardened by the heart-felt truth unsharing,
  Into mere creed.

II

If human eyes be quick to pierce the splendor
 And solve the secrets of the starry skies,
They must irradiate a mind full tender,
  Strong for surprise.

Fair Science binds our inner sight with beauty,
　Philosophy the sluggish brain doth start,—
Varied and lovely makes the path of duty,
　　Nature is Art.

III

Noble must be the motive that befriends us,
　Action alert to follow Heaven's commands;
Never some dream of destiny defends us
　　From life's demands.

So in the mirror of our deeds that cluster
　About us, and our thoughts like stars of night,
No dimness be recorded in their lustre,
　　But growing light.

. . .　Our hearts do burn within us, earth is
　　waning,
　We follow in the way Thy feet have trod,
So would we live the life of Thine ordaining,
　　Thou Man of God.

HERE in the broad fields of the busy West,
  A generous harvest waits the tireless
    hand ;
With peaceful trust the palmy days are blest,
  And sweet, unbroken rest the nights com-
    mand ;
Amid brave toil and hope and courage strong,
  God's ages roll along.

In other lands, the calm expanse of heaven
  Is ofttimes rent by clash and cloud of wars,
To seething strife humanity is given,
  Till pitying earth the ebbing life-tide draws.
Yet who can doubt, serene above the wrong,
  God's ages roll along ?

Whether the glad earth blossom, teem with fruit,
  Or her fond bosom bear the load of death,

Whether the soul in dark distrust be mute,

   Or from its woe give forth melodious breath,

Whether defeat, or victor's joyful song,

      God's ages roll along!

DREAM OF A TOILER

MORN'S varied music
  A child rejoices,
Chanting of brooks and bird-songs
  And faint wind-voices.

Such music woke me
  From peaceful sleeping,
The home-angel hovered near,
  Loving watch keeping;

Her dear arms round me,
  The rose-dawn breaking,
Her sweet accents, "Wake, my child,
  The flowers are waking."

That was the old time!
  Ah, but once only

Can such bliss revisit me
  Toil-worn and lonely.

Once will a twilight
  Bloom into morning,
When hush ! within slumber steals
  Softly—a warning ;

Fore-gleams of heaven
  By dim eyes taken,
God's voice, "Wake, little dreamer !"
  And I shall waken.

LOOKING UNTO SPRING

NOW fade the wreathèd fires of fragrant
    clover,
  Now ebbs the high-tide banqueting of bees,
The purple bloom for heaviness hangs over,
  Nor lures the wing of bird, or lightsome
    breeze.

There falls a burden in the lap of ease,
      While, O my heart,
How hard to watch the flush of joy depart !

Silent the thrushes' deep and mellow numbers,
  Low lies the sun of hope along the West,
The squirrel treads where yet the violet slum-
    bers,
  Her waning life Earth gathers to her breast.

LOOKING UNTO SPRING

Not yet, O Earth, thy deep, foreshadowing rest !
   But why, my heart,
Should seasons move thee, steadfast as thou art ?

Such eloquence abides in blossom lowly,
 In branches bountiful and cool of breath,
So full yon fountain-flow of meaning holy—
 A human good to him who travelleth,

'T is given to look beyond the grasp of death,
   Believing heart,
To be of Spring's awakening the part.

O God, how can we brook thy loving favor !
 The humblest rill doth cheer the solitude,
And shall we, suppliant of Thy mercy ever,
 Forbear to quell the wrong, diffuse the good ?

Only the burden borne, the *self* withstood
   May hope to start
Th' eternal spring of God within the heart !

CHRISTMAS EVE

CHRISTIANS, behold upon this blessèd
night,
Far upward from the yule-log's festive greet-
ing,
The star of peace, the angel clad in light,
And heavenly hosts the *Gloria* repeating !
O world-wide joy, with thee our hearts are
beating !

Christians awake ! there yet is rayless night
In hearts that ache beneath the midnight
glory ;
Bear we to them good gifts, restoring light,—
The least of them,—we know the Nazareth
story,
And we have reached the Christ in all His
glory !

LUX IN TENEBRIS

HOW beautiful is everything but sin !

I wondered if to lives in prison hordes

Any pure morning ray may enter in,—

Lives that unyielding fate no joy affords,

But which, led forth in chains by tens and
  scores,

Are to harsh toil immured and goading guard.

And yet, methought, the dull reluctant doors

Some stray delight of dawn cannot retard ;

Albeit the full daytide should hold aloof,

Still must all nature free itself of night,

Still must the image of the God bear proof

Of His divine command, *Let there be light !*

To each must fall th' allotted destiny—

The greater or the less—nor come to naught

The soul's invincible immortality

Which is our birthright.

                     Vainly did my thought
Aspire to mount yon vast, mysterious wall,
And solve such dread beyond.   Oh, could I ease
One aching load, or lift the heavy pall,
To cheer by word or deed one heart of these—
God's creatures, madly toiling out their lives
In living death—in dearth of all glad things !
Nay, nay ! the Land of Endless Good survives
Wherefrom there flew a bird of sunlit wings ;

It cleared the massive close, while voicing free,
No longer hushed, the universal song !
Some prisoner's answ'ring throb of melody
Blent with the pæan, I know, and borne along
In swift, convincing harmonies was heard
The message I had sought, without, within—
The miracle of morning and the bird.

      How beautiful is everything but sin !

PASSING THE PORTAL

HOW terrible is death !
    The hush, the pall, the farewell softly
      taken,
The sleep mysterious, love can no more waken,
The well-beloved enwrapt in icy calm,
And ours no power to break the cruel charm,
How terrible, how wonderful is death !

How beautiful is death !
All human life doth seem an idle story,
The mortal doth put on immortal glory ;
O Gone Beyond, whose memory endears
A word, a look, recalled with rush of tears !
How beautiful, how wonderful is death !

Beauty and wonder, majesty and awe,
From out the closing dream of life we draw ;

Yet who can say that life and love are ended?

By all sweet hope, though dimly comprehended,

Undying intimations of the soul

Will yet reveal the whole—ineffable whole.

" It doth not yet appear what we shall be,"

We trust ourselves to One more wise than we.

A blinding, speechless joy will take our breath,

And we shall pass the portal which is Death.

HEILBRONN

He that would make life free, true and beautiful should
go to Heilbronn.—SCHUBARTH.

SCHUBARTH, thy words decree swift elo-
      quence!
  An inward light consuming outward thought
  Two-orbed as Virginis by Herschel sought,
Wherein he gave the brighter, precedence
Of sun to its immediate earth. With sense
  Binate and clear, like to this star inwrought,
  Schubarth, thy bold persuasion we have caught
And echoed from our soul's pure eminence.

Like Leon, we impress the land and sea,
  We pilgrims, mocked as by mirage of youth ;
  Yet not in vain our wayfaring, in truth
The Love supreme is with us, crowning peace,
  And the divine Source of life which maketh
      free—
Our Heilbronn, thro' all ages not to cease !

A SUNSET THOUGHT

O RADIANCE mine when day is o'er,
    O sunset reach of thought to dwell
On joys that linger at heaven's door!
And calm the introspective view
Of what is given me to do,
For if I fail, with purpose true,
    God knoweth all, and it is well.

And be it mine at close of life—
    This rapture given, whate'er befell,
Of yesterdays not filled with strife,—
This gleam of the Unlived to lend
Foreglory. *Truth the Godward trend*,
Were imperfected life's great end,
    God knoweth all, and it is well.

www.ingramcontent.com/pod-product-compliance
Lightning Source LLC
Chambersburg PA
CBHW032354020726
47499CB00008B/2742